The Story of Live Dolls

Being an Account of How, on a Certain June Morning

By

Josephine Scribner Gates

Published by Forgotten Books 2012

Originally Published 1920

PIBN 1000349309

THE STORY OF LIVE DOLLS

JOSEPHINE SCRIBNER GATES

BEING AN ACCOUNT OF HOW, ON A CERTAIN JUNE
MORNING, ALL OF THE DOLLS IN THE VILLAGE
OF CLOVERDALE CAME ALIVE

WITH MANY PICTURES MADE AT THE TIME BY

MABEL ROGERS

THE BOBBS-MERRILL COMPANY
PUBLISHERS   INDIANAPOLIS

Printed in the United States of America

PRESS OF
BRAUNWORTH & CO.
BOOK MANUFACTURERS
BROOKLYN, N. Y.

TO MY LITTLE DAUGHTER
CHARLOTTE
WHOSE TENDER DEVOTION TO
HER DOLLS INSPIRED
THE STORY

ILLUSTRATIONS

The STORY of LIVE·DOLLS

"Look, what's coming!" and with a shout of delight the children of Cloverdale village left their play and rushed into the street.

What do you think they saw?

THE STORY OF LIVE DOLLS

A tiny gilded coach drawn by two beautiful white kittens, with reins of blue ribbons covered with silver bells, and through the coach window the face of a wonderful doll. On her head was a jaunty sailor hat, from under which yellow curls danced in the wind as she nodded and smiled at the children on either side.

From time to time she tossed out a handful of bills, which flew about like little white birds and then fluttered to the ground, where they were eagerly caught up by the fast gathering crowd of children, filled with wonder at the amazing sight. They made a

brave effort to keep up with the coach;
but the driver cracked his whip, the
kittens started at a mad pace down
the hill, and with one
last nod and smile from
the doll in the window,
the coach disappeared
in a cloud of dust. The
children watched it out
of sight, then turned to
go back.

But what were
these bills which,
in the excitement,
they had forgotten
and were still

clutching in their hot and dirty hands? Again and again they read these start- ling words, which stared them in the face:

N O T I C E !

ON THE MORNING OF JUNE THE FOURTH ALL THE DOLLS IN THE VIL- LAGE OF CLOVERDALE WILL BE ALIVE!

That was all; and it was to happen to-morrow, for this was the third day.

They looked at one another with eyes growing larger and rounder, and cheeks growing redder than the roses blossoming in the gardens. Then such a chatter began that even the birds had to stop singing to listen.

"I never heard of such a thing!" "How could they?" "Wouldn't it be perfectly lovely?" And suddenly realizing what a blissful thing was in store for them, if it were really true, the children began to hug each other and dance about and squeal with joy, until their various mothers came to the windows to learn the cause of the commotion. When the little ones caught sight of them, remembering that they had not heard the wonderful news, they shouted:

"Let's tell our mammas!" and quickly disappeared.

Janie Bell's home was the nearest. She fairly flew up the steps and tumbled into the door as she said:

"O mamma, it's going to begin to-morrow! Won't it be lovely! A doll came in a gold carriage and she threw this bill, and a boy doll drove the white kittens all covered with ribbons and bells, and it was too pretty. . . . . *Do* you think my dolls could come alive?"

THE STORY OF LIVE DOLLS

Mamma wiped the little hot face and read the bill.

"It does seem strange, but I don't know of a lovelier thing that could happen to a little girl than to have her doll come to life. What a fine time there would be in the doll house!" she said, glancing out of the window at a beautiful little house under the trees. It was just like a real house, with a porch across the front, a real door bell, tiny shades and Swiss curtains at the windows, and a little brick chimney upon the roof.

Janie clapped her hands.

"O mamma, won't it be fine? I can

hardly wait." She flew out of the door and into the doll house.

Each room was in good order, for Janie was a fine housekeeper. Papa had given the dolls' home to her, thinking that if the little girl learned to keep this one in order she would some day be able to take care of a larger one.

She looked at the parlor with its mimic furniture, a sofa, chairs, piano, and a grate where she could build a fire if mamma were watching. Then she went into the dining-room, where the table was set all ready for dinner. How lovely it would be to see the dolls sitting there and actually eating!

In the kitchen was a little range with an oven, and there Dinah, the black cook, was propped against the wall, looking as if she were only waiting for the magic word to set her marching off getting dinner. Her wig would probably fall off, as it was loose, and her leg was broken. Janie resolved to mend her at once, as it would not do to have her come alive in that condition. She peeped into the dear little pantry at the kettles, skillets and shining pans on the shelves, and at the tiny box marked "Cake."

In one corner was an ice box, in another a flour barrel.

Upstairs there were dolls of all ages and sizes; papa, mamma and children. A little baby in long dresses lay in a cradle, and other dolls were sitting and standing about, some dressed and some, I am sorry to say, stark naked. Janie dressed and arranged them all in various attitudes; then, seized with a sudden inspiration, she exclaimed:

"Well, if it is true, we'll have the best time in this little house we ever had, and I'm going to get ready for it."

So she swept it from top to bottom, washed the little windows, tied back the pretty curtains with fresh ribbons, dusted the furniture, made the beds, washed the dolls' faces, mended Dinah's leg and fastened her wig, flitted about from room to room, giving each one a last fond look, and then she locked the front door and hung the key on the branch of a tree, where it was safely hidden by the leaves.

The sun was setting and papas were coming home to their suppers. All seemed as usual, but it was a new and very exciting world to this little mother, for the morning was to bring strange doings. Janie hurried in to eat her supper and to get to bed early.

"It seems almost like Christmas, mamma; I can hardly wait for to-morrow," she said as she kissed her mother good-night. Mamma laughed merrily.

"Well, close your bright eyes, and the birdies will be singing their morning song before you know it," she said. Janie leaned out of bed to kiss her big dollie, who was sleeping peacefully in a cradle by her side.

No dollie ever had better care, for Janie was a kind little mother. She took her to the table for each meal, gave her a lovely ride every day, and at night carefully undressed her and tucked her into bed.

"Won't it be beautiful"? Janie whispered, as she gave the cradle a little jog. But Dollie slept on, quite unconscious of the fact that in the morning she was to be as full of life and dancing gaiety as Janie herself. As for Janie, she hardly dared think about it; for if she once began to imagine what bliss was in store for her, she would never get to sleep.

During the night she dreamed all sorts of things. Toward morning it seemed that she and Dollie were riding in an egg-shell coach, drawn by two downy, yellow chickens; Dollie suddenly stood up and began to sing, frightening the chickens, so that they ran away and tipped over the carriage.

Of course, at this catastrophe, Janie wakened; but her dream seemed to go on, and she still heard a voice singing. Could it be her doll?

She hardly dared move, as she remembered what was to happen to-day. She listened a moment and then peeped out. At sight of her, Dollie held up both arms and said—yes, actually said:

"O you dear little mamma, I am so glad you are awake. I want to come into your bed," and up she popped and climbed in under the covers, and snuggled up exactly as Janie often snuggled up to her mamma. Janie hugged her, but for a moment was too frightened and astonished to speak.

Miss Dollie began to laugh and giggle so loud that papa and mamma came running in.

"It's true, mamma, **it's true!** Look at her!"

"Of course it's true," said Dollie; "didn't the Queen of the Dolls decide that it should be? It had to be true when she said it. But let's get up and dress; you'll be s'prised to see what's happening in the doll house."

Janie gave a little scream of delight, hopped out of bed and scrambled into her clothes. Dollie was quicker than she, and was soon dressed and standing on a chair by the side of the bed; for Janie had to watch and laugh over the funny spectacle of Dollie dressing herself.

"Now brush my hair, please," pealed out Miss Dollie as Janie finished. Janie gave her another hug, as she brushed the brown curls around her finger; then they ran pell-mell down the stairway and raced out of the house.

The family all laughed heartily, for it was a funny sight to see a doll run. They could hardly believe their eyes,

Janie gave a little scream of delight

and **hurried into their** clothes; **for they too were** eager **to see these wonder-** ful doings in the doll house.

As Janie ran across the lawn, she noticed smoke coming from the chimney. She flew up the steps, unlocked the front door and, as she stepped into the hall, beheld the astonishing sight of black Dinah at the toy telephone. She was just saying, "One steak, please," and then she called up the grocery store and ordered a bill of goods that would empty almost any housekeeper's pocket-book.

Dinah paid no attention to the visitors, but swept the front steps, glanced into the dining-room to see if all was ready for breakfast, and then went into the kitchen.

The fire was crackling in the range, and while Dinah waited for the groceries Janie ran upstairs. The dolls were dressing in the different rooms, and mamma doll was trying to make the baby comfortable. Its cries soon brought Dinah up with a cunning milk bottle, all filled; baby took it and nestled down into her pillow with it, just as any baby would who had to be fed in that horrid way. Janie longed to pick her up, but as she wished very much to see Dinah get breakfast, she thought she would wait until another time.

A knock downstairs announced the grocery boy, and Janie went down to find the table covered with little packages containing flour, sugar, coffee, eggs, and everything needed in a real kitchen. She longed to help put the articles in place, but Dinah looked queer and cross, so she didn't dare touch anything. It was no wonder Dinah was cross, for what do you think

Janie had done in her haste the day before? She had put the poor thing's leg on backward, and had pasted her wig on crooked, way down over one ear. So, of course, she wasn't very comfortable.

After putting everything away, Dinah got a dish, broke an egg into it (such a tiny egg, about as large as a bird's), and with a dear little egg-beater whisked it as light as a feather. Then she poured in some milk and added flour, with a little salt and baking-powder. Janie wondered what she was going to make and glanced at the range. "O joy! pancakes!" she cried, as she spied the smoking hot griddle, the size of a small saucer.

Dinah put on the broiler and laid the steak carefully on it, cut a potato into dice and put it into a pan with a little cream; then, with a dash of salt and pepper on the steak (which was soon done to a turn), she placed it on a platter and generously buttered it. When all was ready she rang a toy bell, and the family of dolls filed down into the dining-room.

They seated themselves, and papa served the food. When he carved the steak the knife bent double, for it was really never meant for use.

"Why, I must go and buy another. I didn't know it was so poor," said mamma doll, as she poured the coffee into the tiny cups and added cream and sugar.

How funny they all looked, sitting there and really eating! Janie tried to smother a hysterical laugh, and made such a queer sound that they all looked up. She felt almost disgraced when her big doll, who had followed her about, whispered:

"Come away, or you'll hurt their feelings."

And now came Dinah with a plate of cakes about the size of a penny.

She poured the coffee into the tiny cups

Each doll clamored for one. How good they looked! Janie ran to the kitchen; she *must* bake those cakes.

"O Dinah, please let me. I will be very careful."

"Well, Miss Janie, you may; but I am cross to-day. My hair is so crooked, and look at my leg! How could you put it on backwards? I have so much work to do, and it is so hard to walk."

"Why, Dinah, you poor thing, did I do that? I will take it right off and turn it around. It won't take me more than a minute, and it will soon dry."

Dinah screamed.

"What! Don't you think I have any feelings? How would you like to have your papa break your leg and turn it round, and you sit waiting for the glue to dry?" and with a scornful sniff she hobbled in with another plate of cakes.

When the family had finally finished eating, there was still considerable batter left; Janie begged for some cakes for herself. Dinah consented, and so Janie and Miss Dollie sat down to eat, taking care to save some cakes for Dinah.

It certainly was bliss to watch the butter melt on those beautiful brown cakes, and to pour the golden syrup from the syrup cup, which had come all the way from Boston only last Christmas.

"Aren't they delicious?" said a piping voice.

Janie jumped up and almost dropped the syrup cup. She had been so busy over those darling cakes, that she had almost forgotten about her doll sitting opposite her at table.

"O you precious thing! I never can get used to hearing you talk. How many times I have played tea-party here with you, and had to do all the talking myself!" and she ran round and gave her another hug. "Let's go and tell papa and mamma about the breakfast," she added; but as they stepped outside they found the family peeping in at the window.

"Isn't it fun, mamma? And did you see the cunning pancakes? The mamma doll is actually going shopping because my knives won't cut meat. The baby was really crying, and I must go up and see her," she rattled on, without giving them time to reply, and then ran up the stairway with the big doll tripping after her.

Stopping at the door of the bed-room, she clasped her hands in rapture, for mamma doll was giving baby a bath. It was kicking up its weenty heels, and gurgling and cooing just like a real baby. While mamma was scrubbing, suddenly baby grabbed the end of the wash-cloth. Of course, it cried when she took it away, and then it stopped to listen, for mamma had wound up the little music box.

So the bath went on till baby was all clean down to its little toes, which mamma kissed and folded tenderly in the blanket. Then she dressed it and laid it in its cradle.

Janie made a motion to take it, but mamma shook her head, and whispering that it was asleep, she quietly put the room in order and drew down the shades. The doll children were making a great racket, and mamma called to them to run out and play, so baby could sleep. Janie and Miss Dollie followed.

As they passed through the kitchen, Dinah was just finishing a marvelous pie, as large as a silver dollar, and singing "Der's a good time comin' by and by." As she opened the oven door Janie caught a glimpse of a dear little bird roasting, and oh! how good it smelled! A dish of cranberries was cooling in the window, and as Dinah left the room for a moment, Janie couldn't resist peeping into the ice box. There was a block of real ice, and a pan of milk with cream on the top of it. How she longed to skim it with the little skimmer!

Then she espied a dish of something that looked like custard, which she was about to taste when Dinah's voice startled her.

"What you a-doin' in my ice box?"

"I only wanted to know what that was," said Janie respectfully, for she was a little afraid of Dinah since the leg affair.

"It's for ice cream, an' I'se a notion

ter let you freeze it. I'se got a heap of work dis mornin'."

"O Dinah, may I?" and Janie danced a hornpipe then and there and threw her arms around Dinah's neck.

"You are a dear, and I am sorry I put your leg on wrong. I do wish I could fix it."

"Nebber mind, honey; I couldn't go through wid dat operation nohow," said Dinah, as she got the freezer and chopped the ice into bits, then poured in the custard and left it for Janie to finish.

With her dear companion by her side she worked until the handle began to turn hard, when she knew it was frozen.

"Dinah, can't we lick the ladder? Mamma always lets me."

Dinah said she might, and she dutifully gave Dollie half. She was sorely tempted to get a spoon and taste that in the freezer, as Dinah had left the room, but she knew that would not be honest, so she covered it up and ran into the yard to see the doll children at play.

She was just in time to see, coming slowly down the street, a white, covered wagon, marked in red letters, "Dolls' Ambulance." It was drawn by six white kittens, who moved along so carefully that Janie decided they must have some very sick patients aboard. It halted in front of the doll house, and the little Queen dismounted, saying she was going to telephone. Meantime Janie, curious to see what was within, walked around to the back and peeped in at the little open door.

There she saw a most piteous sight. It was filled with dolls of all sizes, and in such a condition! Arms and legs were off, wigs were missing, and some dolls lay with their poor sightless eyes staring up at her, in such a pathetic

Janie saw a most piteous sight

manner, that Janie could hardly keep
back the tears. One poor little thing
lay apart from the others and was dripping wet. Her companions sobbed
aloud as they told in low tones of how
she was fished out of a water barrel,
stone dead. Not even the Queen
could bring her to life.

Each had some trouble. Some told
of how their mammas had lost their
arms and legs, and how their wigs had
been off for weeks. Some were sadly
neglected, many being wrapped in small
bed-quilts and soiled blankets, as they
hadn't a stitch to put on. They told
Janie that the Queen had appeared

that morning, had gathered them up from their different homes, and was going to take them to a dolls' hospital. She was telephoning now to make preparations for their arrival.

The Queen soon appeared, and their piteous wailing ceased as she hovered over them, soothing this one and that, placing some in more comfortable positions, wiping away tears which were rolling down the cheeks of little handless dolls, and telling them all to cheer up, that they would soon be made as good as new, except the poor dead one, which they would lay away tenderly in some quiet spot and cover

with pretty flowers. The Queen invited Janie's doll to go with them, and
as they slowly departed, Janie looked
so wistfully after them that she called
to her to jump onto her wheel and follow. Janie ran in to ask mamma,
and was soon spinning along after
them.

By and by they turned into a coun-
try road and down a long lane, at the
end of which she saw a high wall. The
Queen told them that it enclosed a
number of acres of land, and that the
place was called the " Doll Farm."

They all alighted before a great gate
and the Queen blew a wee silver bugle

that hung by a silver chain from her
belt. The gate swung open, and when
they had all entered it closed
immediately after them. The
Queen led them up a
path towards a
building
sign   bearing the
                            "The Dolls'
                            Hospital."
Janie was too
much aston-
ished at the sight that
met her eyes to fol-
low. All she could see was an orchard
of low trees, whose branches hung full
of doll clothes, swaying in the cool

morning air. There were tiny under-garments, and dresses of all colors. She reached out to examine a particularly pretty one, and to see just how it was made, when a voice startled her.

"Don't touch that. It isn't ripe yet."

"Ripe!" said Janie. "Is it growing?"

"Why, of course. Now see. The button holes aren't begun yet, and the buttons aren't near tight enough. It will be about two weeks before that frock can be picked. Now here is one I can pick to-morrow," and he explained to Janie just how he could tell when it was ready to be removed from the tree.

Then the gardener, for it was he, showed her the trees full of under-garments and dear little petticoats, the bushes of different colored stockings, with shoes and slippers to match, and last of all, a tree of hats. They were the sweetest things, of many different shapes, and from the end of each branch hung bright ribbons of all colors. Near by grew all sorts of flowers.

The gardener told Janie she might trim a few of the hats, if she cared to, as they were all ready to pick. Now, if there was one thing Janie liked more than another, it was to trim hats. So the gardener picked a number and allowed her to choose the ribbons and flowers.

She chose red, blue, pink and white ribbons, and roses, forget-me-nots, pansies and morning-glories. You must remember these were all dwarf flowers, much smaller than ours, and the gardener told her they were everlasting, and so would not wither.

Janie seated herself under a tree, from whose branches dainty parasols of all colors were dancing and nodding in the breeze. She would have been eager to pick them at any other time, but now with her lap full of such visions of beauty, she was blind to everything else about her. She arranged the bows and flowers, and soon had this lot of hats trimmed, and begged for more. Finishing a number she placed them in long rows on the shelves built for that purpose.

She then threw herself on the ground to rest, and, glancing up, saw the parasols.

She clapped her hands and bounded to her feet.

"O Mr. Gardener, can't I have one?"

He said she might, and asked her which one she wanted.

"That beautiful blue one. No, the pink one. O no, wait a moment, that white one, I think. O, Mr. Gardener, please let me look a moment. They are all so sweet!" She finally decided on the blue—a beauty with lace and forget-me-nots around the top.

The pink one had a wreath of wild roses, and it was hard to give that up; but the blue matched her doll's new dress, and so that decided it. Then the gardener told her that after awhile she could help him pick the various garments for the army of dolls that had just arrived, but that now she'd better go into the hospital and see what they were doing there. And so he led her into the house.

Here Janie found the poor crippled dolls being put in fine shape by little doll nurses, wearing soft gray dresses with white aprons and caps. Legs and arms were being replaced; the blind were made to see with blue eyes and brown; bald heads were covered, and such a wealth of hair did those dolls have—some curly, some braided and

tied with a ribbon, and some hanging straight, for the dolls' mammas to braid or curl, as they chose. When their bodies had finally reached perfection, they went into a bath-room for a sorely-needed bath, and Janie went to help the gardener.

Together they wandered about, plucking an outfit for each doll. It was great fun to match the dresses in slippers and stockings, and then to complete the costumes with the proper hats. When they carried the frocks in, what a hubbub arose! Each doll wanted every dress.

The little Queen quieted them and gave a suit to each one, which they soon put on, and they looked so sweet, clean and pretty that their own mammas would hardly know them. The Queen called for the bill, paid it, and departed with her family, looking like the "Old Woman Who Lived in a Shoe."

They made a very pretty picture as they walked out, appearing like a lot of gorgeous butterflies. As before, the gate swung open at a peal from the silver bugle; all climbed into the ambulance once more, and away they went with Janie following.

When they reached home they found the yard full of little girls weeping for their lost dolls. But as each dollie jumped down and ran to its own mamma, what a chattering and b b-bling filled the air!

"Who mended you?" "What lovely hair!" "Where did you get those clothes?" cried the little girls.

The strange tale which Janie told them of all she had seen, and especially of the clothes growing on trees, seemed too wonderful to be believed, and they envied her such delightful experiences.

THE STORY OF LIVE DOLLS

The little Queen then mounted the steps and gave them a short lecture. She told them how kind they ought always to be to their dolls—just as kind as they wished their mammas to be to them.

She said that when she went from house to house gathering up all the old dollies to have them made like new, she was shocked to see the condition of some of them. One had a hopeless crack in its head, because its mamma got cross and threw it up to the ceiling. Some of them were naked, and most of them were very dirty. Her eyes filled with tears as she spoke of the poor little dead one; and she said she could always tell what kind of heart a little girl had by the way she treated her doll. Those who made the sweetest and tenderest mammas were those who had taken the most loving care of their dollies when they were little girls. She wanted them to begin over, and see who could be the best mother during the few weeks that followed.

Then they all sat on the grass, and Dinah appeared with cunning glasses of lemonade and tiny sandwiches, and they enjoyed this almost more than the lecture. When they had finished the Queen said good-by, telling them to enjoy each other while they could, as this bliss was to last but a month.

Only little girls with live dolls can know of the happiness that followed. It was no uncommon thing to see dolls playing "ring-around-a-rosy" and "hide-and-seek," or jumping ropes and rolling hoops. Janie never tired of watching them, and she and her precious doll had many romps.

Early one morning there was left at the door a miniature invitation, which announced that a picnic was to be held at the Doll Farm the next day. Janie

The dolls playing "ring-around-a-rosy"

ran into the doll house to ask if they would go, and found Dinah busy cooking for it. She had just finished the layer cakes, which had been baked in the lids of baking-powder cans. They were all iced, some with chocolate, others with plain white. A number of tiny square loaves of angel food and sponge cake looked so good that Janie longed to pocket one.

Dinah allowed her to cut out the fried cakes with a thimble, and when they were a golden brown, she rolled them in pulverized sugar until they looked like a heap of white marbles. Dinah then made a batch of cookies, which Janie cut also. Next came a lot of jelly tarts and apple turn-overs, so crisp they would undoubtedly melt in your mouth.

Last, but not least, she made dozens of the dearest little baking-powder biscuits, and when they were baked Janie opened and buttered them and put in pieces of dried beef, shaved very thin. They were delicious. Janie received one from Dinah, and longed to swallow a dozen.

Then Dinah boiled a number of eggs, for which Janie tied up packages of salt and pepper, as these are necessary for every picnic. She then helped to place the food on the pantry shelf, ready to pack in a hamper the next morning.

How tempting it looked! When they had squeezed lemons for lemonade and frozen the ice cream, they sat down to rest.

Dinah said it was to be a delightful picnic, given by the Queen to all the dolls and their mammas. Every little girl in the village was invited, and she did hope she had enough to eat!

Janie ran home to tell mamma about it, and to ask if she couldn't make something for the lunch. Mamma thought for a moment.

"I know the very thing," she said. "Jump onto your wheel and go to each little girl's house, and tell her to be here at three this afternoon, and to be sure to wear an old dress."

"You are the darlingest mamma!" Janie cried, as she hugged her and ran away with a delightful feeling of mystery. "It must be lovely if mamma planned it, but what *can* it be?"

Promptly at three all were on hand. Mamma took them to the kitchen.

"We will make some doll candy, and I will show you how," she said.

They had to relieve their excited feelings by dancing a jig at this de-

lightful news, and then they settled down to work. They first made some chocolate drops, the weentiest little things you ever saw; then some marsh-mallows, which were about the size of parchesi dice.

Next they made maple-creams and dear old-fashioned molasses candy, which the children were allowed to pull, and the one who succeeded in getting her piece the whitest was to have a dainty little box of the mixed candies.

It was great fun! When it was finished it looked so good that mamma had to divide a box among them. Then she brought out the popper, and the children went gaily about shelling the corn. This is always a delight to pop, and when they had a heaping dish of it, they made it into popcorn balls about the size of marbles.

While they waited for the candy to harden they ran into the garden to play and to talk over these strange happenings.

"O children, what lovely times we are having!" said Janie. "I wish they could last always." And each one piped in:

"Yes, but they can't, and we must enjoy them while they do last."

"I know one thing, I do take better care of my doll now. I never used to keep her face clean, and she was nearly always naked."

"It was mine that was ruined from my throwing her up to the wall. I was so mad at her that day, just because I couldn't make her dress fit. I have a new one now, and I am very careful of her."

"And mine was drowned, but I really was sorry after I did it. She wouldn't stand up, and I grew cross and threw her into the water; but, of course, I never knew she had any feelings. There goes my new one now, riding the wheel which papa had made for her."

The girls clapped their hands with delight at the unusual spectacle. To think of a doll on a wheel! What would happen next?

Just then mamma's voice summoned them to the kitchen, where they found a great basket of little candy boxes in the forms of hearts, diamonds, half-moons, drums and cunning barrels. They packed the candy neatly and tied each box with a pretty ribbon.

Then the boxes were placed in the basket, ready for the morrow, and the little girls departed for their homes. The next day proved to be fine, and soon after break-fast the children and their dolls were assembled in Janie's yard.

They were clad in pretty dresses, and looked as sweet and fresh as a lot of daisies.

Then appeared two tallyhos, the one for the dolls being drawn by four curly white dogs. The Queen's own boy-doll driver snapped the whip, and the air was at once filled with the noise of the barking of the dogs and the music of the bells on the harness of the restless steeds.

The tallyho for the children was much larger, and was drawn by four sream-white ponies.

They were all packed in like sardines in a box, the little Queen sitting in the midst of the dolls. The silver bugle was blown, the chains and bells jangled, and away they flew.

They were barely started when they heard Dinah calling. She was frantically waving a red bandanna kerchief and beckoning them to come back. So back they went.

"You done forgot me," she shouted.

"You! Why, Dinah, are you going?" asked Janie.

"Co'se I is, and I don't like to take no liberties nor nothin', but I feel like I must tell you dat you done forgot anodder t'ing dat I consider mighty impo'tant ,to ebery picnic, and dat is de lunch what I'se been workin' at dis long time."

This speech caused a hearty shout of laughter. Mamma came to help put in the hamper and baskets, and Dinah sat in state by the driver. With her red kerchief on her head and her yellow dress, she looked like a great bumble-bee hovering over the dainty doll flowers.

As they rode away, mamma heard her singing her favorite song, "Der's a good time comin' by and by." Perhaps she was thinking of the time when her leg would be turned around, or, perhaps, of how much they would enjoy the toothsome luncheon she had prepared. They had a fine ride, as it was a beautiful day, and they were all so perfectly happy.

They sang and shouted, and were envied by all the boys in the village, who were deprived of these pleasures because boys are so dreadful in their treatment of dolls.

All too soon was the ride at an end. The girls were eager to see the trees where the dolls' clothes grew, and when they were actually inside of those wonderful grounds, they ran here and there like ants. The Queen first led them around to her own home, which Janie had not seen when she was there before. It was the dearest little place, with climbing rose vines twined about the doors and windows, and was beautifully furnished with everything one could wish for.

The Queen's own bed-room was like fairy land. The bed had Swiss curtains draped about it, tied back with blue ribbons. There was a lovely desk filled with tiny doll-paper and envelopes, and a little gold pen and a cut-glass inkstand. Here she had written those gracious invitations.

The closet was filled with beautiful little dresses. A shoe box held various colored shoes and slippers, also bed slippers and a dear little pair of rubbers. On the dresser was everything any young lady could desire. It was charmingly arranged with a lace cover over blue, and a dainty pin cushion, silver comb, brush and manicure set.

In one corner stood a book case, filled with books of the tiniest sort. A long window led out into a balcony; here was stretched a doll's hammock, where one could swing and pick flowers without moving, for the roses twined in and out.

After this they went to see the hospital, and then to have some games with the dolls. They examined the trees carefully and found them most mysterious. Lunch was called before they dreamed it could be time, and, as that is always the best part of a picnic, and as little girls are always hungry, they hurried to the spot where Dinah was serving.

Every mamma sat by her own doll, and as the food was passed each doll helped herself, but the poor mammas were like the little pig that had none, as they were not allowed to take a morsel; and to make it worse, what do you think those saucy dollies did? Have you ever had a dolls' tea party?

Have you ever had a dolls' tea-party?

Then you remember how you held the food to your doll's mouth, pretended to let her have some, and then gobbled it up yourself.

Well, that is just what happened here. Each doll held it to her mamma's mouth, and, as she tried to take it, it vanished in the doll's mouth in the most irritating manner. Every time Dinah passed the same performance followed, and how the dolls laughed!

The children grew hungrier every moment when they found those tempting viands were not for them. The ice cream looked so delicious! It was strawberry, and served in small saltcellars; and then came that lovely angel food and jelly tarts. They coaxed and pleaded, but the dolls only said:

"That's the way you treat us at your parties."

Finally, when they were on the verge of tears, the dolls relented and Dinah brought in a fresh supply, which vanished very quickly, as everything was unusually good and the children were nearly starved.

When they had finished, they presented the dolls with the boxes of candy, and wound up with a merry game of hide-and-seek.

THE STORY OF LIVE DOLLS

The old gardener called them and said that each little girl was to be allowed to choose one entire suit for her doll. What a scramble they made for the various trees, though it was very hard to decide, for everything was so pretty.

Janie looked a long time before she could quite make up her mind, but finally chose a pink dress with pink stock-

ings and slippers, and a hat with ele-
gant pink plumes waving upon it; a
fan and chatelaine completed this cos-
tume. She chose also the dear pink
parasol she had so much wanted before. There were also stunning coats
and opera capes with swan's-down
trimming, and one tree full of dear
little muffs.

The handkerchief tree looked too
funny, with the tiny white things flut-
tering about like a flock of birds with
wings spread ready to fly.

It was a hard matter to leave this
enchanting place, but as the sun was
getting low they gathered up their bas-

kets, presented the gardener with some of their candy, and with many thanks and good-bys departed.

When they reached home they told the Queen they never in all their lives had had such a beautiful time, and, thanking her very heartily for giving them so much pleasure, they went to their homes "to tell mamma all about it."

The days flew merrily by, and before they realized it the month was almost gone. When Janie stopped to think of those happy times being no more, she was ready to cry her eyes out, but she put away the thought, determined to enjoy them while they lasted. One morning at breakfast papa said:

"Mamma, I think we must wind up these remarkable doings with something pretty fine. How would it do to hire several carriages and take the whole caboodle of these chicks, with their wound-up dolls, for a lovely day at the seashore? The various mothers, or rather grandmothers, of the dolls can go to see that they don't get drowned. It is only a drive of ten or twelve miles to the beach. You can get dinner at the hotel. I will telegraph and have that arranged for. You

can all have a plunge in the surf, and
the babes can dig in the sand and pad-
dle about, and have no end of a good
time. How does that strike you,
J ```"

Janie replied by springing into his
lap and giving him a hug that almost
choked him.

"Oh, that will be lovely," she cried,
"and I will write the invitations."

They decided to have it the very
last day of this eventful month. Janie
wrote the notes which were to make
so many hearts happy, and papa went
to make the necessary arrangements.
The day came, and Janie sprang out

of bed to raise the shade. Instead of seeing the sun streaming in, as she hoped, she found the rain was pouring down in sheets. She made a brave effort to keep back the tears, as she heard her dollie singing the well-known song, "Can't we Make Sunshine in the House when there is None Without?"

"But, Dollie, we can't go," sobbed Janie.

"Why not?" came from mamma's room.

"Because it's raining, mamma," and then the tears began to fall in earnest.

"Rain before seven, clear before

eleven," sang papa. "Don't borrow trouble, Polly love, but get dressed and see what will happen."

Janie dried her eyes and obeyed, very much surprised, for she was seldom allowed to go anywhere in a rain like that.

After breakfast mamma got out waterproof and rubbers, which Janie put on, and then waited patiently for what would follow.

The door-bell rang and a package was left for Janie's doll. On opening it she found another tiny package marked on the outside, "Not to be opened until you reach the beach."

There was also a little gossamer and a pair of rubbers, which fitted Miss Dollie to perfection. How charming she looked!

Janie hopped about like a young robin, as she heard the delightful blast from the trumpet, which was always associated with their good times. She rushed to the window and saw, drawing up in front, two omnibuses, one filled with the various mothers, the other with the little girls and their dollies. But what was this procession which followed?

"Oh, mamma! it's all the dolls from the doll-house, and each has on a tiny

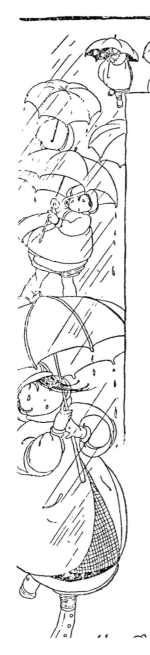

gossamer. How funny they look!" And so they did, each carrying an umbrella and paddling through the water. Mamma, Janie and Dollie followed them, and all jumped in the omnibuses, closed the doors with a bang, and away they went.

It was snug and cozy inside. The rain pattered on the roof and played a steady accompaniment to

the chatter of this jolly little crowd,
which looked so odd, hooded and
cloaked in black, like so many nuns.
The little mammas cast many admir-
ing glances at their dolls, for they had
always longed for them to have these
wee rainy-day garments.

"Isn't it the greatest fun?" they
cried. "I'm so glad it rained; it's
much nicer to be shut in here and
listen to it," and they hugged one another in their delight.

They had a merry ride. The Queen
*t*old some delightful stories, which
were so interesting that when the sun
broke through the clouds they never

noticed it; till, the last story being finished, they all shouted in one breath:

"Look at the sun!"

And now they found they were nearing the beach. They could hear the ocean roaring, and could see the waves creeping up and rolling over with that great swish, which once heard is never forgotten, and is sweetest music to lovers of the sea.

The 'buses stopped, then all tumbled out and made a mad rush for the water. Oh, the beauty of it all! How sweet the air was! Who can breathe that delightful, salty odor and not love it? They played in the sand and gathered shells until eleven o'clock, when the air was warmer, and mamma said they might put on their bathing suits.

"But what will the dollies do?"

Janie's doll waved her mysterious package, and every other doll waved one also, crying:

"Wait and you will see."

Then all disappeared in the bath-houses; the girls hurried into their suits and awaited the dollies' reappearance with the greatest impatience. When they finally came they pranced around them and cried, "Oh, you darlings, where did you get them?" And no

wonder, for they were clad in the gay-
est little bathing suits you ever saw,
with all the colors of the rainbow.

How pretty they looked skipping
about! They had a merry game of
tag, while waiting for the dolls' grand-
mammas to disrobe, and made a beautiful picture, dotting the sand with
dainty bits of bright color. At last

all were ready, and they plunged into the surf. Such fun as they had!

The storm had made frothy, snowy waves, which came in faster and faster, tumbling over each other, as if to see which would reach the shore first. The children and dolls took hold of hands and rushed in among them, only to be hurled back in one confused mass of legs, arms and heads. For a moment it would have been hard for an on-looker to tell just what it was, but the tangle soon unraveled, and the performance was repeated with an ac-companiment of wild shrieks of laugh-ter, as the waves rushed over the heads

of dollies, children and mammas. The mammas were soon tired out and sat on the beach to rest and watch this performance on nature's stage, and, as the waves tossed the children and dolls out on the sand, they laughed till the tears ran down their cheeks.

Some of the dolls were left standing on their heads, others walking about on their hands, and one poor little doll was stuck in the sand, with one leg and an arm sticking up in the air. They helped her out and she ran into the water again, undaunted at such a slight mishap. At last they came out breathless and lay down on the sand to rest before dressing.

They looked so funny, that mamma told them she ought to do with them as did an old lady that she once heard of, who allowed her children to play near a little stream which ran by their home. When they fell in she hung them on a line and fastened them with clothes-pins, stuck through their toes. It was so odd to see them hanging in a row—ten of them! When they were dry she took them in, sprinkled and

ironed them, and let them loose again. They were hung so low it really didn't hurt them, and they thought it great fun.   One day she left them hanging while she went to the store, and a thunder shower came up.   She rushed home in a panic and, of course, found them dripping.   She took out the clothes-pins, shooed them into the house like a brood of chickens, gave them each some ginger tea and hustled them into bed, piling blankets upon them till they were nearly smothered. They recovered, of course.

"And now," said mamma, "we must get dressed and go to dinner."

They all had a hearty laugh over this remarkable tale, and thought mamma would have to have a great many clothes-pins and a very long line upon which to hang them.

When all were ready they walked up to the hotel, where the guests were eagerly waiting for them. They had seen the telegram which ordered din-

The dolls ate a hearty dinner

ner to be prepared for thirty mothers, thirty children and thirty live dolls, and they watched with the greatest interest the little girls, each with a doll by her side, march into the dining-room. How astonished they were when they saw the dolls eat—actually put food into their mouths and swallow it. That was the strangest thing! The dolls weren't a bit embarrassed, however, and ate a hearty dinner and enjoyed it, too, for the long ride and the bathing had given them fine appetites.

After it was over they filed out, and the guests after them. The grown people begged the mothers to tell them what it all meant, and their children surrounded the little girls and their dolls. Of course, the story that they heard was very strange and hard to believe, but they could see this part of it with their own eyes, and so could not but believe the rest.

All too soon came the omnibuses to carry them home. They were to have a pleasant open-air ride this time, as the roofs had mysteriously disappeared. With many good-bys they departed, leaving the guests with much to talk about. This had been another beautiful time, and it seemed a fitting end to the month's jubilee; but Janie couldn't be quite happy, when she remembered it was the final act in this strange play.

"Dear little Queen," she pleaded, "couldn't you let it last just a little longer? We can't bear to give up these good times so soon."

"My precious child, this must be the end for the present—I always keep my word, and the month will be up in the morning; but," she added, as the tears sprang to all of those bright eyes, "if you take good care of your dolls and try to be helpful to your mammas, I will let it happen again some day, and you may then have even a better time; so do not grieve. Remember, dear little ones, I love you with all my heart, and will plan something even more beautiful than this has been."

And now she bade the driver stop at the Doll Farm, where was waiting the same wee coach which had so startled them at the beginning of this remarkable month. A little trunk strapped on the back said plainer than words that these times were truly at an end. Giving each a loving good-by kiss, and begging them not to be unhappy, the Queen jumped into the gay little coach and was whirled away. The children were driven to their

separate homes, each hugging her doll
and loath to give it up to its former
existence. Janie tried to brighten up,
as she bade them all good-by, and said:
"It will happen again. The Queen
said it would, and it will; so we ought
to be extra good. We have had a delightful time and must be thankful for
it, and just think what we have to look
forward to!"

That night she tucked in her dollie
as usual, and, after one last fond kiss
and a few extra caresses, was soon in
the beautiful land of dreams, where we
will leave her till the "next time,"
which, as the Queen always tells the

truth, must surely come some day. Perhaps it will be in the winter, when they can have merry sleigh rides and snow-ball battles. And perhaps, as we listen to the chimes of the Christmas bells, if we peep through a window of the doll house, we shall see a tiny Christmas tree and "stockings hung by the chimney with care," and even hear dear old Santa Claus' sleigh-bells, the reindeer pawing on the snowy roof, and his great voice crying, "Merry Christmas to all, and to all a good night!"

That would indeed be a perfect time, so we will not be sad at bidding the dolls good-by, but, as the curtain falls on this act, sing with dear old Dinah, "Der's a good time comin' by and by."